SCELIDOSAURUS

(ske-LI-doh-SAW-rus)

TYRANNOSAU...

(tie-RAN-oh...

TRICERATOPS

(try-SER-a-tops)

PTERODACTYL

(TER-oh-DAC-til)

STEGOSAURUS

(STEG-oh-SAW-rus)

APATOSAURUS

(a-PAT-oh-SAW-rus)

ANCHISAURUS

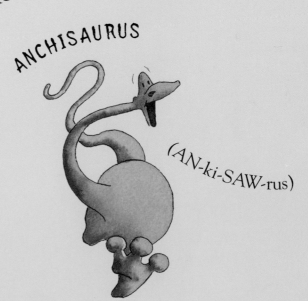

(AN-ki-SAW-rus)

This

Harry

book belongs to

. . . .

More Adventures with
Harry and the Dinosaurs

Ian Whybrow and Adrian Reynolds

PUFFIN

PUFFIN BOOKS

Published by the Penguin Group: London, New York, Australia,
Canada, India, Ireland, New Zealand and South Africa
Penguin Books Ltd, Registered Offices: 80 Strand, London WC2R 0RL, England

puffinbooks.com

Contents

Harry and the Dinosaurs at the Museum

Harry and the Dinosaurs Go Wild

Harry and the Dinosaurs go to School

Harry and the Dinosaurs make a Splash

Harry and the Dinosaurs make a Christmas Wish

Harry and the Dinosaurs at the Museum

Sam wanted Mum to take her to the museum.
She had to study the Romans for homework.
"What are Romans?" asked Harry.

Sam said they were our ancestors, but he was
too young to understand.
Harry wanted to take the dinosaurs to see them.

Sam said, "No way!"
She said Harry would just get bored and silly.
That was why Sam's homework got smudged.

Mum made them both settle down.
She said a museum would be a fine
outing for everybody.
  "I'd love to go," said Nan.

The museum was bigger than a hospital.
You had to have a map.

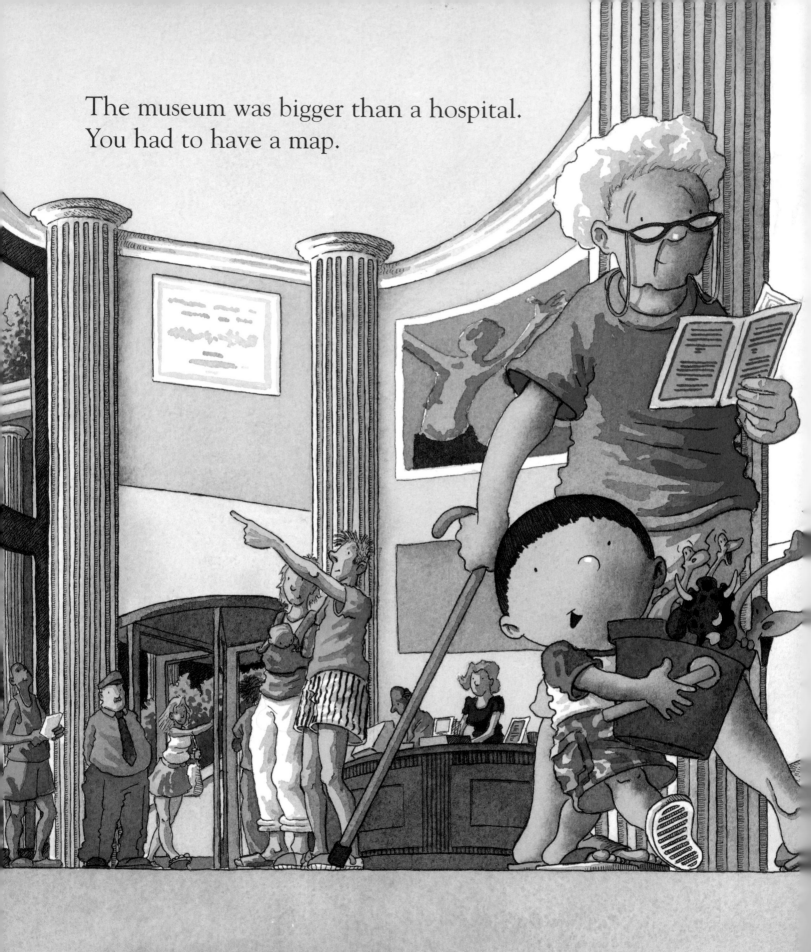

On the way to the Romans, they passed the cavemen.
  "Are these ancestors?" asked Harry.
  Mum said yes, everybody in the world came from cavemen.
  They lit fires and did hunting.
  Harry liked the stone axes!

The dinosaurs liked the
sabre-toothed tiger!
Raaah! Sharp teeth!

Next stop was the Egyptians.
  They saw mummies in boxes and funny
writing like pictures.
  "Are Egyptians ancestors?" asked Harry.
  "Yes, but not the right ones," said Sam. "We
want the Romans. Come on, hurry up!"

Finally they reached the Romans.
They had good swords and spears,
and helmets with brushes on.

But what a lot of old pots, broken ones too!
　Sam started doing drawing.
　"We've seen the Romans now," said Harry.
"I'm hungry! Let's go!"

"Raaah! Anchisaurus pinched me!" said Stegosaurus.
"He's taking up all the room!" said Anchisaurus.
"Behave!" said Harry in a loud voice.
"Look, Harry *is* being silly!" groaned Sam. "I knew it!"

"I think the dinosaurs need a run about," said Harry.
 Mum said better not. They might get lost.
 "Come on, let's get something to eat," she said.
"Afterwards we'll come back here, so Sam
can finish her studies."

The cafeteria was very busy. Nan and Harry and the dinosaurs waited at a table while Mum and Sam went to queue up.

"Look, I'm a caveman! Raaah!" said Triceratops.
"Look, I'm a Roman! Raaah!" said Pterodactyl.
"Look, I'm a mummy! Raaah!" said Tyrannosaurus.

After lunch, everyone felt a lot better and they
set off back to the Romans.
But it wasn't long before Anchisaurus got bored.
"I'm bored too!" said Tyrannosaurus.

"Never mind," said Harry, "it's your turn to do studying. Pay attention, my dinosaurs."
He taught them Climbing Up Display Cases.
Then taught them Sliding On The Slippery Floor.

That was how they got lost.

"Oh no! Where's Harry?" said Mum. "Quick! Let's find the person in charge!"

Sam said Harry was stupid. "I bet he's gone off on a bus!" she said.

"Nonsense!" said Nan. "I know where we'll find him!"

They followed Nan to the Prehistoric Hall. "There he is!" said Nan. "I knew it!"

Harry was still teaching his dinosaurs.
"Boys come from cavemen and Romans and Egyptians,"
he explained. "But these are *your* ancestors."

So Tyrannosaurus said "Raaah!" to his ancestor.
  So did Apatosaurus and Scelidosaurus and Triceratops
and the rest of the bucketful of dinosaurs.
  All except Pterodactyl, who gave his ancestor a nose-rub.

"Now, young man!" said the person in charge.
"We had better look for your mum. Could you
tell me your name?"

Harry said his name, address and telephone
number, no problem at all.
All the people said very good, clever boy!
Nan rushed over. "He's with us!" she called proudly.

"Harry!" said Mum. "We thought we'd lost you!"

"I wasn't lost!" said Harry. "I was with my dinosaurs."

"And we were with our ancestors," said the dinosaurs. RAAAAH!

ENDOSAURUS

Harry and the Dinosaurs Go Wild

It was a long drive to the safari park but it was worth it.
Apatosaurus saw an animal just like Triceratops.
"That's a rhinoceros," said Harry.
"Triceratops has got more horns."

Mum liked the giraffes best and Nan
liked the zebras.
    The monkeys were funny but the
man said not to feed them.

Sam asked him if they had pandas but the man
said no, they were endangered animals.
Harry wanted to know what endangered meant.
Sam said he was too little to understand.

Nan helped. She bought Harry a book about endangered animals. She thought it was sad about the Sumatran tigers. People kept hunting them so there were only a few left in the whole world.

Harry really wanted to help but he had no money.
  "I want to save some animals," he said.
"What can I do, Mum?"

Sam said, "Tuh! What a waste of time!"
   She said he was miles too small to make any
difference. That's why Harry made her do a smudge
with her lipstick.

Mum took Harry off to settle down.
Then they looked on the Internet
and found lots of endangered animals.

Mum said why not do a poster? Harry could put it up in his window. Then maybe other people would help the animals too.

Harry liked that idea. He got out his drawing stuff straight away. Trouble was, it was hard to know which animal to save first.

The dinosaurs said, "Raaaah!
We want to save some BIG animals!"

So they started drawing.

Tyrannosaurus did a polar bear.

Pterodactyl asked Harry to help him do a gorilla.

"Wait till I've finished my blue whale," said Harry. "Blue whales are bigger than trains, bigger than dinosaurs, bigger than thirty-two elephants!"

Stegosaurus did an army tank.
"Army tanks don't need saving!" said Triceratops.
"Do a tree frog instead."

Mum said the drawings were excellent.
She helped put the words on.
LET'S SAVE THESE ENDANGERED ANIMALS!

Nan said, "Why not talk to Mr Bopsom?
He might put up a poster in his shop window!
Then people can see the pictures when they go shopping!"

Mr Bopsom loved the pictures but he thought they might be a bit too small for a poster.

He asked Harry if he could draw them bigger.

Harry said no, sorry, his pictures always came out small.

"That's a shame," said Mr Bopsom. "Because saving animals is important!"

Poor Harry. He went home feeling maybe Sam was right. Maybe you had to be big before you could be any use.

The very next day, Mr Bopsom was on the phone.
"I've had an idea!" he said. "Can you do me *lots*
more pictures?"

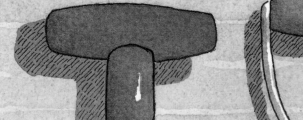

So Harry and the dinosaurs did more birds
and bugs and reptiles
and *lots more dinosaurs!*

Then off they went to give them to Mr Bopsom.

When Harry went into the shop two weeks later
he was amazed! Mr Bopsom had made all the
drawings into cards.
  He said that every time somebody bought a card,
some of the money went to save endangered animals.

Everybody loved them. They said, "Marvellous!"
  "What a brilliant idea!"
  "So original!"
  "Four cards for me, please!"

The lady from the paper came and was very impressed.

"What a wonderful thing you've done!" she said.

"Raahh!" said Apatosaurus. "Save the strawberry poison arrow frog!"

"Raahh!" said Pterodactyl. "Save the teeny blue tongued skink!"

And Harry said, "Quite right, my dinosaurs! Because even if you are as tiny as a tick on the tail of a green turtle, you can still do something that makes a BIG difference!"

ENDOSAURUS

Harry and the Dinosaurs go to School

It was a big day for Harry. He was starting at his new school.
He was very excited because one of his friends, Charlie,
was starting that day too.

Stegosaurus said he didn't want to go. Not after
Triceratops told him about no Raaahs in class.
Mum said not to worry, school would be fine.

Harry blew his whistle just like a teacher.
   He said, "In twos, holding hands, my dinosaurs.
No talking and jump in the bucket."

The dinosaurs did what Harry said.
   All except Stegosaurus. He was so
nervous, all his plates were rattling.
   Harry had to give him a special stroke.

Sam said, "You can't take dinosaurs to school, stupid!"
That's why her toast fell on the floor.

Mum took Harry to school.

Mrs Rance was waiting at the classroom door when
Harry and Mum got there.
  "Hello, Harry," she said. "Welcome to your new school."
They all said goodbye to the mums and dads.

Then Mrs Rance showed Harry the coat pegs.
    "You can leave your lunchbox here too," she said.
    Harry was too shy to say could he have his bucket back.
    That's why his dinosaurs got left outside the classroom.

Harry missed his dinosaurs, so he didn't like the classroom.
He didn't like the home corner, or his special work tray.

And he felt sorry for another new boy with a digger
who cried when his mum went home.
The boy wouldn't say one single word, not even his name.

Harry sort of liked the playground at playtime.
But it wasn't much fun, even the monkey bars –
not without his dinosaurs.

Back in class, the digger boy still wouldn't speak.
  "Maybe he wants to go to the toilet," Harry suggested.
"I'll show him where it is, shall I?"
  Mrs Rance said good idea, how thoughtful.

All the way to the toilet the boy kept quiet.
  It was the same on the way back, till they got to the coats.
Then they heard a voice, very sad and very soft.
  "Raaaaaaaaaah!" it said.

"That's my dinosaurs," said Harry. "They miss me. Would you like to see them?"
    The boy nodded so Harry said, "This is my Apatosaurus and my Anchisaurus and my Scelidosaurus.

This is Triceratops and Tyrannosaurus. Pterodactyl is the baby.
Wait! Where's Stegosaurus?"

"Jump out, Stegosaurus," called Harry. "Don't be shy!"

But Stegosaurus wanted a whisper.

"Ah," said Harry. "Stegosaurus says he will come out but only if he can have a ride on your digger."

And do you know what? The boy nodded and passed it over.

When Harry and the boy got back, Mrs Rance said,
"Oh good! Dinosaurs. I love dinosaurs. Do they Raaah?"

"RAAAAAAAAAAAAH!" said the dinosaurs
and blew all the windows open.
   "My goodness!" said Mrs Rance. "That *was* a Raaah!"

They all sat down in the classroom.
 "Now, we're going to make new labels for our coat pegs," said Mrs Rance. "Hands up who knows how to write their name?"

The boy with the digger put up his hand.
"And what are you going to write?" smiled Mrs Rance.
"Jackosaurus!" said the boy.
It was the very first word he had spoken all day.
And what a good joke, too!
All the other children laughed and laughed.

Harry felt very happy.
　Charlie, Harry and their new friend Jack sat down together at a table with the dinosaurs.

They laughed and they Raaahed
and they made beautiful labels
to show where they belonged.

ENDOSAURUS

Harry and the Dinosaurs make a Splash

Harry and the dinosaurs loved the wave pool at the indoor Water World. Jumping over the waves with Sam was FUN!

Then a big wave came and knocked them all over!
That spoiled it! That wasn't nice at all. The water
made them cough and got in their eyes.

"Raaah!" said Anchisaurus. "This tastes terrible, Harry!"

"Raaah!" said Triceratops. "Our bath at home is much nicer!"

"Quick," said Scelidosaurus. "Let's run away!"

So Harry and the dinosaurs ran back to Nan.
  "Why don't you come in this pool?"
she said, but they didn't want to.
  "Raaah! We hate water now,"
said Tyrannosaurus.

Nan said, "What a shame them old
waves spoiled things for you. Let's see
if something cool will help."

She took them for some juice and double scoops of ice cream with extra sticky stuff. Ahhh! That helped a lot!

"Are you ready to go swimming again now, Harry?" asked Nan.

Harry wasn't sure. "My dinosaurs don't like getting splashed," he said. "But maybe they'll go in if you come too, Nan."

Nan looked worried.

"I'm ever so sorry," she said. "I haven't been swimming for years. I expect I should sink like a stone!"

Sam said it was stupid coming all this way and then
being too scared to go in.
That was why Nan threw a bucket of water over her.
"Mind your own business, Miss Cleverstick!" she shouted.

Harry took Nan to settle down.
  "You're not allowed to splash people in swimming pools, Nan!" he told her.
  Nan said quite right, shocking, she was ashamed of herself.

So Harry and the dinosaurs took her to watch the people on the water slide.

Nan thought that looked tree-mendous!

"Why don't you try that, Harry?" she said. "Sam would take you, I'm sure."

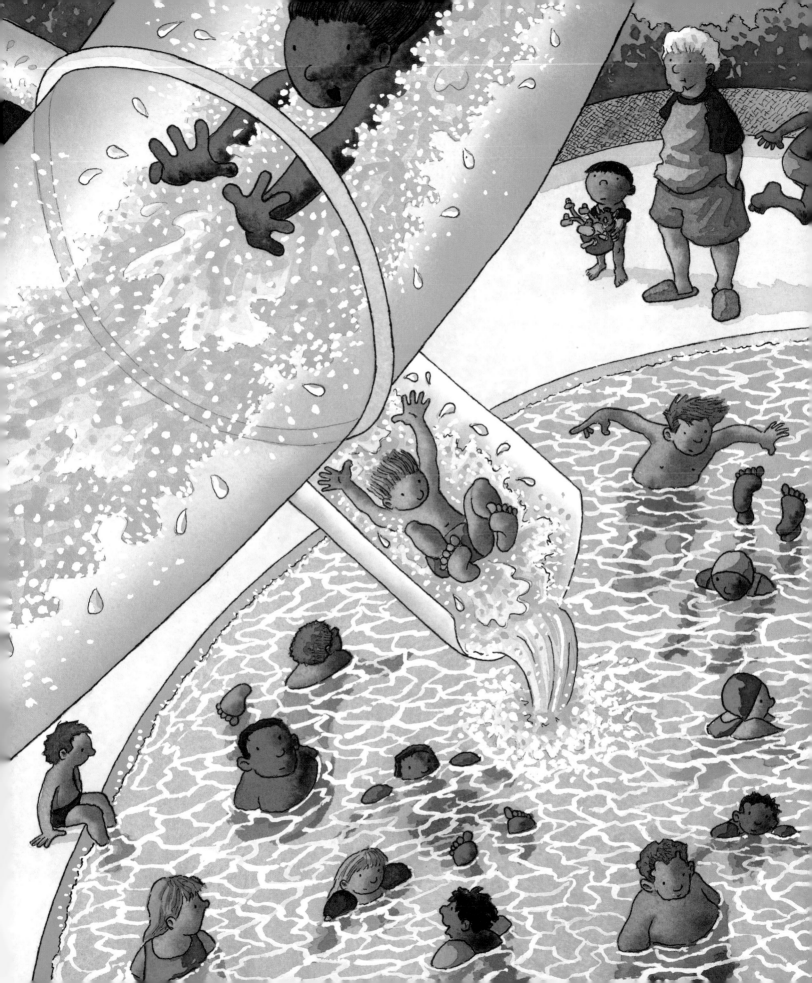

It *did* look really fun, but Harry and the dinosaurs didn't feel *quite* brave enough yet.

"Raaah!" said Apatosaurus. "We don't want to go with Sam!"

"We only want to go with you, Nan," said Harry.

"That's ever so high . . ." said Nan. "But I suppose we'll be all right if we stick together!"

She grabbed Harry's hand and they rushed off to the shop.
Nan chose a bright yellow swimsuit for herself and some
goggles for Harry.

"Here, pop these on," said Nan, "while I buy myself some
senior armbands."

"Let's go!" said the dinosaurs. "If Nan
can do it, we can do it!"
They climbed right up to the top and
they were only a little bit scared.

What a surprise for Sam!
Nan and Harry and the dinosaurs
made the biggest SPLASH of the day!

"Cool!" laughed Sam. "And I thought you you were scared of the water."

"I was nervous, that's all," said Nan. "But Harry's helping me."

"And my dinosaurs!" said Harry. "They're helping too!"

"Raaah!" said Pterodactyl. "I'm a dive bomber!"
"We like rough waves now," said Scelidosaurus.
"Look, we can bite them!"

"How do I look?" laughed Nan. "Am I sinking like a stone?"
"No, you're definitely swimming!" said Harry and the
dinosaurs. "You look tree-mendous!"

ENDOSAURUS

Harry and the Dinosaurs make a Christmas Wish

It was always fun to visit Mr Oakley's farm. One time, he
had some ducklings keeping warm in a box by the stove.
Harry took the bucketful of dinosaurs to see.

Mr Oakley showed them one little duckling just coming out of its shell.

Harry even held the duckling in his hands.
"Raaah! Ask him, Harry!" said the dinosaurs.
"Ask Mr Oakley for a duckling to keep."
Mr Oakley said better not. They only had room
for chickens over at Harry's house.

Mr Oakley let Harry and the dinosaurs ride home
in his trailer, but they were still upset.

"Shame," said Triceratops.

"Raaah!" said Tyrannosaurus. "We want a duckling!"

"Oh I *wish* we could have one!" said Harry.

It was a big wish, but it didn't work.

Maybe it was the wrong time for wishing.

At last, one cold day in the winter, the right time came.

Nan said, "Harry, will you and the dinosaurs help me stir up the Christmas pudding mixture?"

They all had a good stir and a lick – and
then they closed their eyes and they made
a *special* wish, a Christmas wish!

Harry wrote down his wish in a letter to Santa.
"What did you wish for?" asked Mum.
"A duckling!" said Harry and the dinosaurs.

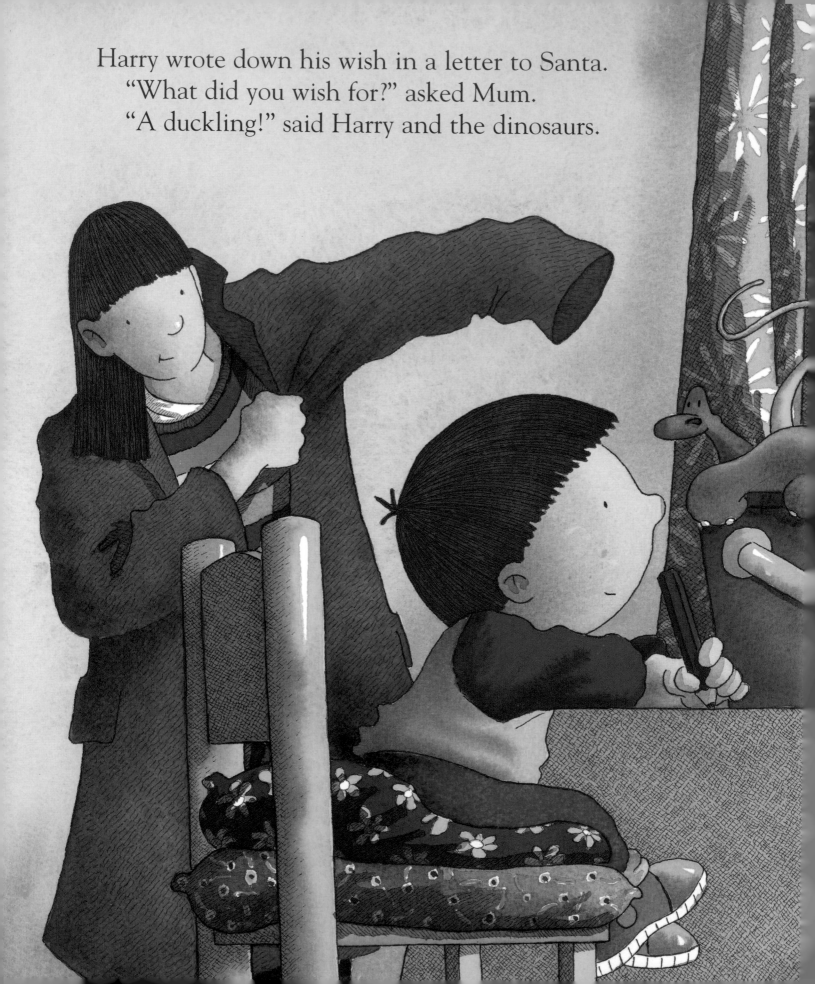

"Well . . . let's look in the shops before you send that letter," said Mum. "Just in case you change your mind."

"Good idea!" said Nan. "I want to spend my savings out of my egg money box!"

They all went on the bus to see the lights and
the Christmas displays in the big stores.
Harry found just the right book about
dinosaurs in the bookshop.

And there was plenty Harry liked in the toyshop!
So he thought of lots more things to put in his letter.

"But don't forget to say about our duckling, Harry,"
whispered the dinosaurs.

On Christmas Eve, Nan helped Harry to hang up his stocking.

"Dinosaurs don't like presents in stockings," said Harry.
"They want their present in an egg."

"I see," said Nan, "then we'll leave out my money box, shall we?"

Sam said it was stupid putting out an egg.
Eggs were for Easter, not for Christmas.
That was why Harry and the dinosaurs made
RAAAH-noises all through her favourite programme.

Nan took Harry to his room to settle down.

"I've been bad to Sam, haven't I," sighed Harry.
"Now I won't get my Christmas wishes."

Nan said not to get upset. Christmas wishes were special,
and if you were really sorry, Santa would understand.

When Harry opened his eyes
it was Christmas morning!
   "Wake up, my Apatosaurus,
my Anchisaurus and my Triceratops!" called Harry.
   And he called, "Wake up," to his Stegosaurus
and his Scelidosaurus and his Tyrannosaurus and
all the sleepy old dinosaurs.
   They jumped up and rushed downstairs
to see what Santa had left for them.

Harry unwrapped all his presents.
"Just what I wanted!" he shouted every time.
    "What a shame," sighed the dinosaurs.
"Santa didn't bring us a duckling."
    "Wait!" said Harry. "You haven't opened your egg yet!"
    So all the dinosaurs closed their eyes, gave the egg a
warm-up and made a Christmas wish.
And guess what popped out . . .

...a baby pterodactyl!

"Raaah! Much better than a duckling!" said Scelidosaurus.
"Raaah! It's a flying dinosaur!" said Tyrannosaurus.
"Raaaaah to you too," said Pterodactyl.
Happy Ch-raaaaah-stmas, Harry!

Meet Harry and his bucketful of dinosaurs!

TYRANNOSAURUS

PTERODACTYL

SCELIDOSAURUS

STEGOSAURUS

TRICERATOPS

ANCHISAURUS

APATOSAURUS

HARRY
(HARRY-oh-SAW-rus)